Published in Great Britain in 2022 by Mascot Media (Norfolk) for Rosie Andersen.
Email: mascot_media@btinternet.com   Web: www.mascotmedia.co.uk

© 2022 Rosie Andersen Web: www.aelfwynnbooks.com

Illustrations © Paul Jackson Web: www.pauljacksonstory.com

A CIP catalogue record for this book is available from the British Library.

ISBN: 978-1-7397144-0-6

Rosie Andersen has asserted her right under the Copyright, Design and Patents Act, 1988, to be identified as the author of this book.

Design, layout and editing by Marion Scott Marshall and Alan Marshall (Mascot Media).
Printed by Swallowtail Print, Drayton Industrial Park, Taverham Road, Drayton, Norwich, Norfolk NR8 6RL.
Email: contact@swallowtailprint.co.uk   Web: www.swallowtailprint.co.uk

CONTENTS

PREFACE

In the story of *The Swan and The Golden Hare* I have drawn inspiration from, and woven together, a number of myths, legends and themes.

Firstly, the legend of the Swan-Maiden, forms of which appear all over the world. Following on from this, the stories around Wayland the Smith, including his association with swans. I have also included the concept of the daemon, the carrier of our destiny, and the phenomenon of Will-o'-the-Wisp, a shape-shifter, which appears in both English and European folklore – or, as he is sometimes known, Jack-o'-Lantern. Here in East Anglia, there is the curious legend of a fearsome and ghostly black dog, known as Black Shuck, notorious for his demonic appearance in both Bungay and Blythburgh churches. Finally, within all of this, I wanted to explore the themes of fear: ambiguous and disenfranchised loss; grief; courage; and, finally, freedom – and how these might be incorporated within the folktale genre.

As a location I have chosen the lost Suffolk hamlet of Hethern, which, according to the evidence that exists, may have been situated on the road between Dunwich and Blythburgh, set within marshland near Walberswick. Over many centuries the hamlet would slowly have ceased to exist after the decline of Dunwich as a major medieval port. With this in mind, I have set the story in the mid-15th century to include the character of William de la Pole, the infamous Earl of Suffolk, who by 1450 had become the most hated man in England.

ROSIE ANDERSEN

THE SWAN AND THE GOLDEN HARE

Swans in the winter air
A white perfection have

W.H. AUDEN, FISH IN THE UNRUFFLED LAKES

INTRODUCTION

My name is Edric, and I am the son of Ralph, the Miller of Hethern. I am also a teller of stories. I have always had a vivid imagination, encouraged by my father and my grandfather before him, both of whom were inspired and visionary storytellers.

Storytelling describes tales of everyday life – ordinary, and sometimes extraordinary. They speak of happenings and experiences portraying all manner of things, including love, loss, hardship, adventure and evil, most always combined with a hefty dose of mystery and strange occurrences.

As a storyteller, I was invited to Stonehill Castle near the hamlet of Hethern to entertain a favourite of King Henry VI, William de la Pole, Earl of Suffolk. The imposing castle overlooking the marshes was not only home to William for several months of the year, but also to many of his own favourites, whom William invited most often for advantageous political reasons. The company was lavishly and extravagantly hosted, and I was there to amuse and divert, for which I was handsomely rewarded.

What follows is not one of my usual stories of myth and folklore but, instead, I recount here to the best of my ability an honest portrayal of one particularly strange, exceptional and unforgettable winter, a tale that I believe may become a legend.

The Earl of Suffolk, whom I knew well, was not a popular man, particularly later in his life when corruption, misconduct and dishonesty crept in. There was even talk of him orchestrating a murder to further his political career. Could the disappearance and possible death of Humphrey, Duke of Gloucester, have been caused by devilish entities living within the marshland, or was there meddling of another kind? We will never know for sure as William got his comeuppance only three years later in a rather gruesome way.

However, this is not just a story about political corruption – far from it. This is a tale about a beautiful swan called Svanna who overcomes her difficulties, faces her loss and grief, and thereby finds courage and freedom.

So, dear reader, look carefully between the lines; be curious, explore and let your imagination run wild.

CHAPTER 1: SVANNA

Broad-hipped, wide-winged and feather white

It was a peculiarly wet season when Svanna, a tiny cygnet, came into this world. Sheltering under the down-like safety of her mother's weighted wing, she watched the rain pouring relentlessly down. Not far away from their nest, the hamlet of Hethern lay huddled within marshland known as Pallifen. It was a land of mystery and, at times, of danger; a watery world of wind-wafted reeds that shimmered gold and silver in the ever-changing light. Pallifen was believed to be haunted by a Will-o'-the-Wisp or, as he was known to the villagers, Jack-o'-Lantern, who, if feeling mischievous, with his flickering lights in the dark of night, would lure lost travellers to their deaths.

Crisscrossing the fen, channels of murky water provided refuge to the creatures that inhabited the area, and where the locals placed their eel traps woven from the flexible reeds. Close by, a track made its way through the wetland, crossing the land by means of a heavy stone bridge, and in the near distance the imposing Stonehill Castle stood tall overlooking the marsh below. The castle was the residence of William de la Pole, Earl of Suffolk, who came each year to hunt with a party of his favourites. They were times of excessive decadence and rich feasting, with William having a particular liking for swan meat. It was well-known amongst the swan population that every year their healthiest and most handsome would disappear, destined for the Earl's banqueting table.

Svanna, one of five cygnets, stood apart from her siblings in that her plumage, instead of the dull, grey-brown of early life, was already pure white, a difference that would soon attract attention. Svanna was mostly silent, solitary and a little ungainly. Although in her own mind her thoughts were lucid and meaningful, 'Fear' prevented her from expressing these in ways that others might understand. Her siblings teased her for being too sensitive, finding loud noise and bright light uncomfortable. She preferred the shelter and soothing calm of her mother's care, although she was now getting too big to be cosseted. In order to escape the mayhem of family life, Svanna would look for the quiet backwaters of the marshland, swimming gleefully around with her wings stretched upwards, breathing in the clear and refreshing air that made her feel calm and at peace.

As Svanna grew, unlike her siblings who were more interested in bickering with each other, she was entranced by the beauty of her world. During the harsh winter of her first year of life she deliberately kept away from the squabbling to observe the wonder and fragility of her surroundings: the hostile east winds tousling the tops of the reeds and spinning the surf into hazy droplets; the shadows tumbling into the dank, dark waterways; and the yellow-ochred lichen clinging to the exposed salt-tinged trees. Even the clouds appeared to cling perilously to the winter skies, swirling and scattering into wispy lines that reflected, striped and snaked into the watercourses below. It was a cold, raw landscape, but to Svanna it was perfect.

CHAPTER 2: SKIDDADLER

Amber-wrapped, black-tipped and sprint-legged

Since the loss of his beautiful swan wife Allwise, who, being disillusioned with mortal life, reclaimed her bird form to fly away to freedom, Wayland the Smith had remained true to his word by never again causing mischief amongst the swan community. Over the aeons, he had, from his tombed home, devoted his time to shoeing the occasional horse of passing visitors; but, more importantly, to being a carrier of others' destiny.

One day, Wayland, upon hearing news of the arrival of a vulnerable pure white cygnet, was filled with compassion for her troubles. In order to help the young swan overcome her plight, he knew that he must act soon before she became too grown-up where her adult restrictions and duties would get in the way of her soul's purpose. Wayland, being a skilled, elvish shape-shifter, and so as not to alarm the sensitive cygnet, chose to become a distinctive golden hare called Skiddadler. Whilst Svanna was growing up, the prophetic golden hare visited her frequently in her dreams so as to foretell her adventures. Svanna regularly dreamed of becoming a Swan-Maiden and a rescuer of creatures that found themselves in danger. For a while her dreams allowed her to escape into a place of adventure and safety, a release from her sensitivities. It was a way of making sense of her world.

As time passed, Svanna, the small and awkward cygnet, grew into a graceful adult swan. She met Sven, a handsome cob, and they made their home together, living peacefully amongst the reeds of their watery world; and, in doing so, Svanna temporarily forgot the voice of her destiny. Their life was tranquil until one terrible day when everything changed.

CHAPTER 3: THE HUNT

It was one of those mornings when the mist hung motionless in thick, opaque bands as if suspended by invisible threads. A strange, eerie silence permeated the marsh, the wind having dropped to a nothingness. Sunrise had arrived, but the day was reluctant to begin. The incoming tide had started to encroach on Svanna's nest, which she and Sven had skilfully and elaborately constructed out of dried grasses, sticks and rushes, and which sat safely on a dry mound camouflaged within the reedbeds. All that could be heard was the gentle lapping of the water as it passed through the twigs and rushes of their nest.

Sven was already out foraging when Svanna was suddenly filled with a sense of unease. With little notice of any impending danger, a horn sounded, cutting through the still air. Svanna froze in fear, as the horn sounded again, this time accompanied by voices. Her thoughts immediately went to Sven. "Where is he, is he in danger?" flashed through her mind. Birds flew up in alarm, and the squeals and squawks of other creatures could be heard. Out of the misty stillness four men appeared, wading up to their waists in water, pulling small skin-covered boats. They were wielding axes and knives, hacking at the reeds looking for prey. The men, one of whom Svanna recognised as the Earl, were on a mission to capture swans to be taken to the castle enclosure and kept until ready to be despatched for the banqueting table.

Suddenly a heavy net engulfed Svanna; she was pinned down with the weight of the trap that crushed her slight body. She tried to raise her wings but was unable to do so. She fought against the heavy mesh until she was breathless, her chest heaving and painful from the exertion. With her determined thrashing she gained her chance, quickly diving to free herself of the entrapment, swimming under the water to a safer distance away until her lungs were fit to burst. With all her strength, and amidst the shouts of the hunters, she flapped her wings, paddled desperately, and at speed fled in terror along the waterway until she was elevated in flight. From a safe height she was able to observe the mayhem below. She caught sight of Sven, who was unaware that he was being ambushed by the hunters, and they were closing in on him. She tried calling out to Sven to alert him to the danger, but it was no good. Just at a time when she needed her voice, 'Fear' had slipped in to prevent her making any sound. It was too late; the net was hurled and Sven was caught. The hunters tied him up; all four men were needed to hold Sven tight and carry the strong bird back to the castle.

Once the coast was clear Svanna descended, falling to the ground gasping, landing awkwardly back into the water. Her old adversary 'Fear', which had so often repressed her voice, had allowed her to escape the hunters with her life, but cause Sven to be captured. Svanna was not only gripped by grief but also by guilt. Sobbing, as she tried to paddle back to the nest, an intense pain overwhelmed her. She looked for the source of the agony – her foot, twisted and distorted, was hanging loose and lame. How she had managed to swim at all was a miracle. She dragged herself slowly back on to the nest, exhausted from the effort of staying alive. That night she slept fitfully, any rest torn apart by horrifying dreams.

Svanna did not know whether Sven was dead or alive, although she felt certain of his ultimate fate. Through her grief and loneliness she wept and wept. Her tears poured, cascading endlessly, filling the dykes to overflowing, causing the low-lying land to flood, the streams to become torrents, and turning her intricately constructed nest into an island.

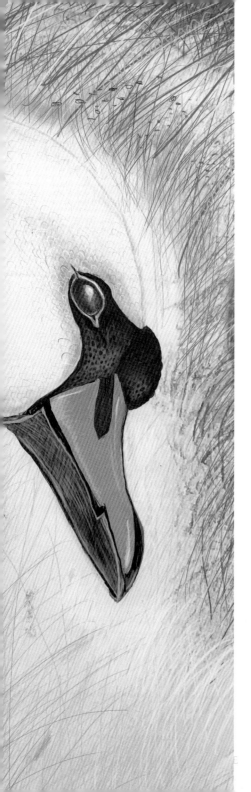

CHAPTER 4: DESTINY

In periods of great sadness time appears to stand still; but, as we know from experience, it cannot be stopped, and time passes, as it inevitably does. Grief changes everything. It cannot be set right, or made to go away on demand, for grief has its own rhythm. Svanna's life had indeed changed. It had become vague and confusing, with a veil that cast a desolate shadow, obscuring any clarity. This prevented any joy from entering, and it felt to Svanna as if the grey gloominess would last forever. Only occasionally would she catch a glimpse of brightness that would momentarily lift her spirits, evoking memories of happier times.

Wayland the Smith, being aware of Svanna's plight, sat despairing at his tombed home waiting for the right moment to intervene. He knew he must act fast to guide Svanna towards her destiny. But first he must help her to restore her strength, and so he decided he must visit her personally.

One morning, in his disguise as the golden hare, Skiddadler swam across the water to Svanna's nest, carrying food with him. "Good morrow, Svanna," Skiddadler announced. Svanna, though surprised at the hare's boldness, sensed a familiarity and was unafraid of this strange visitor. "Good morrow to you," she replied. "My name is Skiddadler," the hare said. "There are murmurs in the vicinity that you have suffered an injury, and are unable to swim or fend for yourself."

Svanna gently began to tell Skiddadler her story, recalling it carefully, the memory of which still felt too close for comfort at times. "In my attempt to get away from the hunters," she said, "I must have broken my foot. I have not been able to swim or find food, and have only eaten worms that I am able to catch from my nest. My strength has gone," she cried. Skiddadler then unwrapped the bundle he had been carrying. Carefully, unfolding the woven reed pack, he revealed a veritable feast of little fish, frogs, molluscs, algae, weed and insects. "My, thank-you!" she said, tucking into the food with delight and gratitude.

Skiddadler stayed for a while and listened. Svanna explained, "Sven and I knew the dangers of the Earl coming regularly to the castle where he liked to hunt for swans. We grew up knowing this and that any one of us could disappear, never to be seen again. We heard from the humans living in the village and who worked at the castle that the Earl is renowned for holding lavish banquets where swan is the centrepiece of the feast. But, of course, you put these awful thoughts out of your mind as best you can, and get on with living. I never expected Sven to be captured."

Then Svanna said quietly, "Nobody told me about how the loss might make me feel. "You see," she went on, "swans bond for life; if we lose our mate, we can die of a broken heart. Other animals here at the marsh are unable to grasp this and have little compassion for my plight." Skiddadler kept listening, his heart full with care and concern for her. She continued, "When we lose someone we love, it is normal to mourn and grieve, but I do not know whether Sven is alive or already dead. Everything is unclear and bewildering. There is no conclusion, and I feel as if my grief is frozen in time; that I have to keep my grief hidden from those who don't understand."

Every day Skiddadler returned with food, and every day he stayed to give Svanna comfort and to listen to her. Slowly her injury healed and she began to swim again, returning to that unbridled freedom of her cygnethood, paddling the waterways, away from the intrusions of others. She was once again able to absorb the sights and sounds of nature, the hues and tones of the coast, from the glimmering, gleaming light to the whispering of the waves lapping the pebbles. She listened to the ebbs and flows; the smell of the waterways and the nearby saltiness of the sea where the mewing gulls dived and darted with aerobatic freedom. All of this distracted her from her deep sorrow.

Skiddadler felt that the time had arrived for Svanna to move towards her destiny. One night he revisited Svanna in her dreams, where she dreamt once again the youthful dream of becoming the Swan-Maiden, shedding her bird form, inhabiting a human guise with pearlescent skin and raven hair. Yet, unlike most mere humans, Svanna possessed a perceptive intuition that allowed in-depth insights into situations and circumstances.

CHAPTER 5: OTTER

Velvet soft, attentively whiskered
and cinnamon-eyed

Svanna's dreams became more and more lucid, with that state between night and day more indistinct, more vague and more ephemeral; the veil obscuring what is real and unreal.

On one particular night Svanna was jolted awake by a sense of panic and calamity. Her intuition sensed danger. She rose from her nest, immediately diving into the water beneath, swimming with urgency but also with grace and fluidity. She noticed her body. She no longer had feathers but soft skin covering sleek and lithe limbs. She had transformed into the maiden who appeared in her dreams.

The cries that awoke her became more insistent. She swam following the sound, which led her to an otter, whose leg was trapped and entwined in strong weed. The otter was held fast beneath the water, her life fading. As quickly as she could Svanna untangled the mass of vegetation to release the distressed creature. Once set free, but before the otter swam away back to her holt and her kits, Svanna, sensing there was something more to be said, curiously asked, "Otter, tell me who you are". The otter replied:

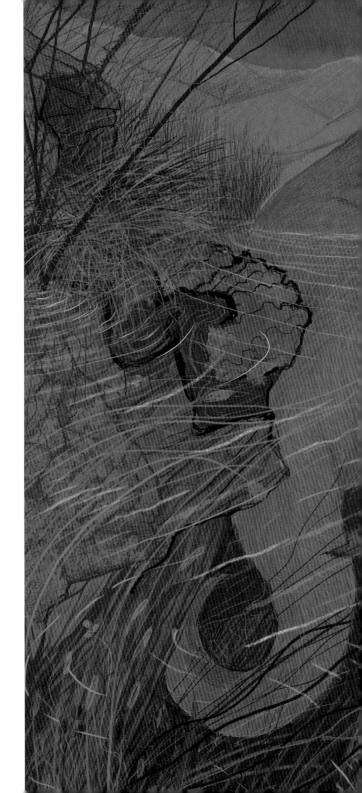

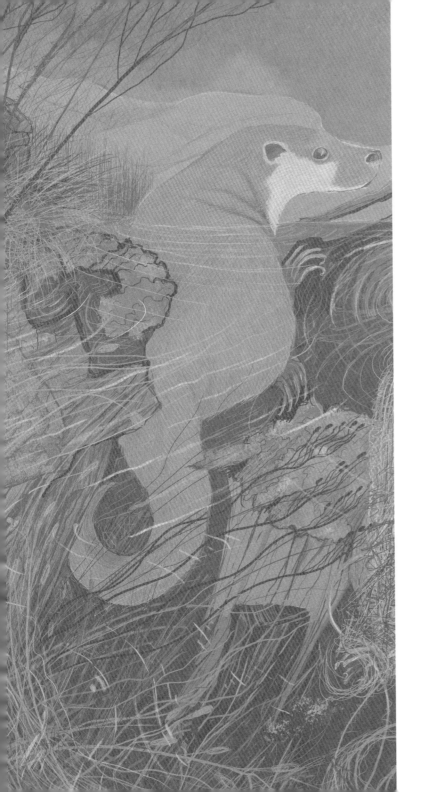

"I am indeed Otter, but my true name is Fear, and
I have always been your companion it seems.

Though I originally came to protect and
alert you to life's dangers,
due to an unexpected twist of fate at your birth
I have become the thorn in your side, your nemesis.
Unintentionally, I became the night-stalker,
the demon lurking at every corner;
the creeper; the nightmare.
I became your foe, your adversary, your undoing,
and I have at times been destructive,
misplaced, illogical and irrational.
I have been adept at exaggeration.

I am here to tell you, Svanna, that those unhelpful
fears can be vanquished
and you will triumph over them."

At which point the otter disappeared into the night.

The next morning Svanna awoke as normal in her warm and sheltered nest with what she thought was a dream, still so fresh in her mind. She looked down at herself, half expecting to see skin, arms and legs instead of feathers and webbed feet, but 'no', she was just her usual swan-self, other than a mysterious black whisker sticking to her otherwise pure white plumage, and to which she paid little attention. "I must have been dreaming", she thought, and got on with her day – but with a little more ease than before. However, those words uttered by the otter remained firmly in her mind.

CHAPTER 6: DIPPER

White-bibbed, pertly curtsied and midnight-attired

Grief is overwhelming and all-consuming. Svanna had moments of guilt, anger, confusion, shock and disbelief at what had happened to her beloved Sven. Her friend Skiddadler had helped her not to give up, and so she knew she must continue with her life – after all, she still didn't know whether Sven was alive or dead. It had been some weeks now since Sven and the other swans had been captured, and there had been no further sign of hunting parties from Stonehill Castle.

Svanna's dreams continued. That night she was once again startled awake with a foreboding sense of imminent danger. As the Swan-Maiden her instincts took over as she dived into the dark depths of the gloomy waters below. She swam following the cries that eventually led her to the bottom of a stream where a tiny dipper lay motionless. The little bird had been knocked unconscious by a rock-fall whilst returning to its nest under a nearby waterfall. Svanna moved the rock, gently taking the lifeless bird in her hands, stroking its tiny body until it began to breathe again. Coughing and spluttering, and so grateful to be alive, the dipper prepared to fly back to its nest. But first, Svanna, aware that the little bird might have a message for her, asked of the bird, "Dipper, tell me who you are". The dipper replied:

"I am indeed Dipper, but my real name is Grief,
and I am not unfamiliar to you.

My true nature is as a power for good,
and to be a supportive companion,
because I only come to those who have loved deeply.
For grief is the unavoidable consequence of love,
and it is far better to have had the experience of love than not.
Be heartened, Svanna: love doesn't disappear;
we carry it with us for all time.
Our grief never ends, either, but it changes.

Now is the time for us to become friends,
and to travel alongside each other for a while longer.
I will take your hand and guide you through this fragile journey of life,
where we will learn to express our feelings as one,
and to carry the pain of loss.
Together we will find a way forward,
and I will travel beside you, always."

With her words spoken, the dipper flew away.

The
following morning
Svanna rose as usual from the
comfort of her snug nest with the
events of the previous night still very clear.
It had all seemed so real, and she had to check
again whether she was in fact still her swan-self.
She did, though, notice an unexpected black feather
clinging to her white plumage. She dismissed this
as nothing unusual, preparing to get on with her
day with a little more contentment than before.
"Another dream", she thought, yet the words
of the dipper remained firmly in her
mind.

CHAPTER 7: SALMON

Moon-silvered, leapingly gallant and dashingly speckled

Over the days and weeks that followed Svanna reflected on her life and particularly on Sven. She missed him, and her heart yearned. She knew she must find the strength and courage to keep going to find out the truth of what had happened to him, to be brave, whatever the outcome. "Courage will prepare me", she thought.

That night Svanna was again woken from a deep sleep, hearing the exhausted cries of a fellow creature in danger. Without further thought she dived into the ink-black waters below her nest to follow the mournful sound to the shallows of a nearby river where a handsome salmon lay gasping for breath, exhausted after numerous attempts to scale and leap the torrents. Svanna gently took the large fish in her hands, lifting it clear of the rapids so that its spawning journey could be completed. The salmon, with gratitude, paused to gain its strength; but before leaving Svanna once again asked inquisitively, "Salmon, tell me who you are". The salmon replied:

"I am indeed Salmon, but my true name is Courage.
Sometimes I am found in unimaginable places.
I can be daring, intrepid and determined but, most importantly,
I have first to believe in myself.

"You see," Salmon continued, "courage is not all about physical bravery;
it can be quiet, passive, silent and solitary.

Standing up tall for what you believe in,
showing strength in the face of pain or grief,
are all humble acts of courage.

I am here to tell you, Svanna, that you are immensely courageous."

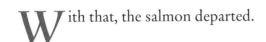

W ith that, the salmon departed.

From the safety and comfort of her bed Svanna rose with the experience
from the hours before still so very distinct in her mind. "Was it all a dream?"
she pondered. Looking down at herself she was still her swan-self, except
she did notice a mysterious cluster of shiny scales sticking to her bright,
white plumage. However, she gave it no further thought. She did,
though, remember the words of courage that had been given to
her, but she knew not from whom. "It must have been another
dream", she thought, and proceeded to get on with her day
with more calmness than before.

CHAPTER 8: JACK-O'-LANTERN

It was early in the year of 1447 that William, Earl of Suffolk, and some of his favourites returned again to Stonehill Castle. The Earl, as ever, entertained extravagantly, with no expense spared. They ate sumptuous meals and drank wine and spirits to excess. They lived off the fat of the land, very often to the detriment of the villagers. The Earl's company continued to spend their days in gluttony and slothfulness; they were proud, contemptuous and arrogant. When they had the energy they would partake in hunting for sport. The villagers, of course, were greatly needed during these times of extravagance to serve at the castle; to cook, clean and attend to the aristocrats' every whim and command; being at their constant beck and call. However, the Earl's party were never grateful and, more often than not, disdainful of the villagers, treating them with disrespect. This caused much resentment. But all was not lost; Jack-o'-Lantern was paying attention and planning his revenge!

The marshes of Pallifen, an extensive area of wetland with drained, fertile areas for growing crops and grazing, provided good food and sustenance for the villagers of Hethern. Woodland lay adjacent to the wetlands where deer, boar and many other animals lived. The area had few paths, known only to the locals. It was very easy to become lost and confused, and even the villagers were wary of travelling in the dark where Jack-o'-Lantern could pounce at any time. However, he was far more interested in those folk who were unfamiliar with the area or who were dishonest or demonstrated little integrity.

After a night of excessive feasting, one of William's party, Humphrey, Duke of Gloucester, known for his recklessness and for being unscrupulous and ill-tempered, left the safety of the castle without a servant to get some fresh air and clear his head. Unable to walk steadily, he stumbled and staggered around. Having lost his bearings, he soon found himself in a state of confusion. Little did he know that he was becoming easy prey for Jack-o'-Lantern, whose villainous and devilish ways were kindled at the sight of the hapless aristocrat. Humphrey saw in the distance a little light which he followed thinking it might lead him back to the castle. However, it appeared to dance mysteriously, sometimes moving rapidly, at other times remaining stationary. He fell, frequently hitting himself on rocks or boulders, but each time managing to get himself up again, but he was becoming weaker in his drunken state. Now, the impetuous and daredevil Duke was not feeling quite so bold or plucky and was fast becoming cold, tired and disorientated.

Suddenly, he heard an ungodly howling coming from different directions. Spinning round and round, with sweat pouring from his face, the terrified Duke tried to run, but to no avail. Jack-o'-Lantern was leading him to his death. Suddenly, a huge black creature leapt towards him with burning, red eyes. The Duke, helpless to defend himself, yelled, then screamed wildly, but the beast's attack was swift and fatal. The Duke was pushed into the water, never to be seen again.

Since the disappearance of Humphrey, Duke of Gloucester, the atmosphere amongst the residents of the castle was somewhat subdued and sombre. Search parties had been sent out to look for Humphrey, but no clues to his vanishing had been found other than some strange burn marks on the wooden supports at Stonehill bridge. The villagers, although themselves cautious of Jack-o'-Lantern, and aware of what might have happened, deliberately exaggerated the stories of Jack's devilish powers and his ability to show himself in different demonic guises. Hence, tales were soon circulating within William's party of fiendish goings-on, and rumours spreading of a large, black and howling beast inhabiting the marsh – the size of a horse, with huge fangs and burning red eyes. For many days the party lay low, rarely venturing out of the castle walls.

Whilst the company was so unsettled, Wayland the Smith had a plan. As the golden hare he would find his way into the swan enclosure and release those birds that remained. He prayed that Sven would be one of them. So, on one night soon afterwards Skiddadler ran speedily towards the castle and, finding the swan enclosure, slipped through a gap in the wooden fence. Skiddadler was careful to make no noise to alert the Earl and his followers. The swans were being kept in a compound to restrict their movements and to fatten them up for the table. Close by was a pond and a small wooden hut. Skiddadler, finding the large iron bolt on the door, stretched himself up to his full height, and pulled on the bolt with all his strength. The door creaked open. Skiddadler, expecting to find a number of swans, was shocked to see only one swan left. "Sven", he whispered. The swan crouching in the corner looked up. "Is it you, are you Sven?", Skiddadler asked hopefully. Sven replied quietly, "Yes, I am he, who might you be?". "I am Skiddadler and I am here to rescue you, Sven. We must leave now."

As quietly as they could Skiddadler led the way towards the wooden gate of the enclosure, where between them they prised it open and sped away, Skiddadler leading Sven to a safe grove in the woods. Sven asked Skiddadler, "Please tell me, do you know what has happened to my beloved Svanna?". Skiddadler reassured Sven that she was safe. He went on to explain, "I am not actually a golden hare, Sven, I am Wayland the Smith, the Lord of Elves. I lost my own beloved swan wife many aeons ago. I had always hoped that she would return but, although initially happy, she sadly became disillusioned with mortal life and fled away. She took back her swan form which I had originally removed from her to make her my wife. I never knew where she went or what became of her. I had to become content to stay in my tombed home, where if a traveller passed I would shoe their horse in return for a silver sixpence. I then took on the role of a daemon, a carrier of others' destiny.

"It was at the birth of Svanna, who, as you know, came into this world as an 'elfin' cygnet with pure white plumage, that my role of daemon was initiated. It had all been predetermined. I was to aid Svanna to overcome her difficulties in life; and I, having taken the persona of the golden hare, have inhabited Svanna's dreams preparing her to fulfil her destiny."

Skiddadler continued. "Your capture by the Earl and his men was not an accident; it had been pre-ordained in order for Svanna to overcome her fears, to grieve, to gain courage and find freedom. She has one more challenge to overcome before the completion of this prophecy – and that is to rescue you, Sven, though not as a swan but as a human."

CHAPTER 10: YOUTH

Golden-haired, guilelessly honest and opalescently hued

The call to liberate another came to Svanna once more. She heard the cries of distress, but these sounds were different; they were not the call of a creature in jeopardy but a cry for help from another human. "Help me," she heard. "Help me, help me!"

Once more, Svanna as the graceful Swan-Maiden dived into the waters below her nest, swimming strongly with all her might towards the anguished and weakening sound. She found a youth, weighed down by his courtly clothes and boots. Svanna grabbed him by the arm and pulled, but she couldn't move him; she didn't have the strength to hold his weight. He was drowning. She tugged desperately at his clothes, managing to remove the heavy outer coat, and then the long boots, which were pulling the youth downwards. But the young man was struggling, thrashing around, unable to hold his breath any longer. With one more attempt and with all her strength, Svanna pushed the young man towards the surface where she was able to drag him to the bank and to grip a tree root. There appeared to be no life in him. She looked in distress at his pale, cold face. She uttered, repeating over and over, "You mustn't die, breathe, breathe". After what felt like an eternity the young man opened his eyes, coughing and spluttering, and having miraculously survived was eventually able to sit up. Svanna wept out of sheer relief. Before he left Svanna asked him, "Youth, tell me who you are". The youth replied:

"I am indeed Youth, but my true name is Freedom,
and I reside in a corner of your heart.

Here is a space that is free from unnecessary restriction,
influence or judgement;
and a special place to make your own choices.

For it is within our hearts that we can be completely free,
to decide our own futures."

The Youth continued:
"In the outside world full of limitations and conditions
there is no such thing as absolute freedom,
but once we have chosen freedom within our hearts
it will spread out into everything we do,
and will lead to creativity, purpose and much happiness."

"Svanna," the youth whispered, "you have found your freedom."

The youth, expressing deep gratitude to Svanna, then departed.

The next morning Svanna awoke from an unusually deep sleep. The darkness of early morning was rapidly lightening in bands of lapis blue, and a sliver of sun glowing red peeped above the horizon. As the day broke through, the sky brightened to glints of gold, illuminating the marshland, dispersing the early mist. The young man in her dreams, and his near death, was still very much on Svanna's mind, as were the words he had spoken. She thought of the journey she had made, from the time she was a small cygnet to now; where she had come from; what she had seen and experienced; and where she might be going. She also remembered the words of wisdom given to her from the other creatures whose lives had been in danger – the Otter, the Dipper and the Salmon. How much had changed in her life.

She stretched herself as the warmth of the sun embraced her nest. Looking through the reeds that were rattling in the chill breeze, and over towards the bleak marshes, she turned her face towards the first faint rays of the sun's warmth. The gulls were beginning their insistent mewing, and in the near distance could be seen a black-cloaked cormorant standing patiently cruciform. As the haze cleared in patches she saw a familiar shape gliding towards her. Svanna blinked, rooted to the spot, not quite believing what she was seeing, though desperately hoping that it wasn't a mirage. This was no longer a dream, an illusion or a trick of the light. Yes, it was true, the swan swimming towards her was Sven, smiling gently as he came closer. Svanna's joy was boundless. Sven was safe, and they were to be finally reunited.

Wayland the Smith, having returned to his tombed home, sat contentedly at this heartfelt conclusion. "After all," the words went through his mind, "swans bond for life!"

It is told that William, Earl of Suffolk, after the disappearance of Humphrey, Duke of Gloucester, and the rumours that subsequently accompanied his demise, left Stonehill Castle, never to return.

With Pallifen returning to a place of tranquillity, Sven and Svanna lived out the rest of their lives in safety. The castle became a ruin, and the stone pillaged to be used elsewhere.

To this day no one has ever found evidence of the castle other than the hill on which it may have stood overlooking the marsh.

"And now my story told, I take my leave

With my puckish spirit, I will not deceive

For fables true, I recount for pleasure

Within them I trust you will deem their measure.

Slumber well my friends, may your dreams be blessed

free from maleficence and much distress,

of howling devils, dancing lights,

apparitions and phantom sprites.

My steadfast companions I bid you farewell

until we next meet, when only time will tell."

Most Heartily Your Servant,

Edric, The Storyteller

THE END

Also by Rosie Andersen...

A story for the seeker, the adventurer, the inquirer and the curious. At its simplest, it is a tale about walking amongst trees and in woods. In addition, it is about being aware of one's surroundings and noticing the myriad happenings within nature, from the miniscule to the immense.

A tale of adventure and fortitude; about the complexities of human nature and our attempts to conquer our demons. It is also a story about friendship and the soul connection between the enigmatic characters of Leof and Elswyth.

www.aelfwynnbooks.com